The Magician's Hat

Written By Malcolm Mitchell

Art By Dennis Campay

"I've had the pleasure of recruiting and coaching Malcolm Mitchell. He came to the University of Georgia with only one thing on his mind... football! During his time at Georgia, his eyes were opened to a whole new world. Part of that new world is a love for reading... and now he has become a writer! He is still one of the greatest college football players in America, but he is also one of the most well rounded young men I have ever met!"

–Mark Richt

Family Fun Day

at the city Public Library is
a special Saturday
that everyone looks
forward to!

The Library

was known for having cool and exciting events!

For the first time, there was **a magician** named David.

Everyone gathered
around the **magician**
to see him perform.

After a series of tricks, the magician was ready to perform his **favorite trick of all.**

He took off his **magic hat** and began to tell the audience his story.

"When I was your age, my mom received an invitation from the library about **Family Fun Day.**

During the book scavenger hunt I wandered into the **Library.**"

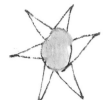

"Out of the hundreds of books, one jumped out at me."

"It was a book
about magic!!
Reading this book
inspired me to become
a **magician**."

"What do you want to be when you grow up?"

Excited, Amy raised her hand and shouted, "**I want to be a dentist!!**"

The magician asked Amy to reach inside the hat. She reached deeper and deeper into the hat until she felt something...
a book.

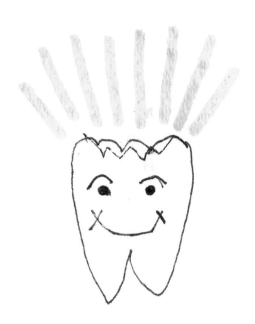

The magician asked Amy,
"What is your book about?"

She screamed, "**It is about teeth!**"

In awe, Matt raised his hand, and blurted, "I want to be a famous **football player!**"

The Magician smiled and held out his magical hat for Matt to reach into.

"Let's see what magic you can find inside."

Matt reached deeper and deeper until he felt something...

Matt roared,
"My book is
about football!"

"Wait a second!
This is not magic!"
Ryan barked from the
back of the crowd.

"Amy's and Matt's
parents must have told
the magician what they
want to be when they
grow up."

The magician challenged Ryan, "**What do you want to be when you grow up?**"

This was Ryan's chance to prove that the magician was fake. So he snickered and said, "**A DOG!**"

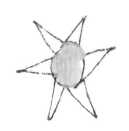

The magician asked Ryan to reach into the magical hat.

At first, he could not feel anything.

So Ryan reached deeper and deeper until he felt something...

Looking at the magician, a puzzled expression flashed across Ryan's face.

The book was not about dogs, it was about **outer space.**

Ryan had always dreamed of becoming an astronaut.

"Whoah," whispered Ryan. "How did you do that?"

"I'm not doing anything," said the magician, "You are."

"I am?" asked Ryan.

"Yes... you. The dreams and desires that are within you created this book.

Follow your dreams, and they will take you wherever you want to go."

The magician
turned his hat so
everyone could see inside.

What are
your dreams?

Special Thanks
Mom, Friends & Family
(Anne, Dave, Georgia, Karly,
Kevin, Lizz, Mike, & Mo')

Malcolm Mitchell is a native of Valdosta, Georgia. He was an Under Armour All-American and one of the most talented athletes in his high school's history. Today, he is considered one of the top wide receivers in college football. He will graduate from college December, 2015.

During his freshman year in college, Malcolm developed a love for reading. Initially, reading was a challenge; however, through perseverance, books became an avenue for expanding his curiosity, creativity, and learning. Today, Malcolm is an avid reader, active member of a book club, and reading mentor to elementary school students.

His inspirational story, which won the College Sports Media Awards' Outstanding Special Feature, has been featured nationally on the CBS Evening News, ESPN, and USA Today, and has been used by many schools as encouragement for students to embrace the importance of reading.

When he is not practicing or playing football, Malcolm can be found in elementary school classrooms across the state of Georgia reading to children.

www.ReadWithMalcolm.com | **#readwithmalcolm – A Lifetime of Learning**

Dennis Campay, a 65 year old artist, began his artistic journey at age 42 after receiving his BFA Degree from the Atlanta College of Art.

During the course of his career he has received numerous awards and accomplishments including recognition for his work from the National Endowment for the Arts. Having participated in over 40 solo and group exhibitions, his paintings are in the permanent collections of museums, universities, corporations and collected by the public worldwide.

With the philosophy that "one should give back what one has received," Dennis is a mentor, teacher, lecturer, and benefactor of the Arts.

Among several publications, The Magician's Hat will be his first children's book. Dennis currently resides in the historic district of San Marco in Jacksonville, Florida along with his wife, Colette, and numerous furry animals!

www.denniscampay.com